KU-775-802

Rapid

Bernard Ashley

Illustrated by Kim Harley

FIC ASH AC029974
NEWCASTLE UNDER-LYME
COLLEGE LEARNING
RESOURCES

A & C Black · London

For Esi Awadzi

With thanks to Esi Eshun, Studio 99,
and David Flower of Abbey Road Studios

The song wouldn't go away: no way could Jonny lose it. The day after Mr Turner's music lesson it was still there – from breakfast through to bed. From the moment Belle had banged out the notes and Charlee had pinned on the words, the song had stuck, *Don't go away*.

But what had done the catching was the face of Win Bhekezulu as she sang it with Charlee and Belle. Win was melody, Win was harmony, Win was symphony. And when she did a quiet Zulu click, throat and teeth on the 'go go go' – chin up, smooth neck –

she's beauty!

That was why Jonny couldn't get the song out of his head; because he'd grown up through school with Win, and now, on the turn of a day, she was knock-you-down special.

6

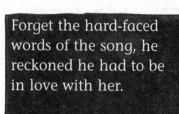

Forget the hard-faced words of the song, he reckoned he had to be in love with her.

Don't get me wrong
Don't go go go away
I want you all night long
Don't go go go away.
But talking true
The fact with you –
Your face is out my head
by light of day.

NOT!

Win's face would never be out of Jonny's head, or out of his heart. The thought of Win Bhekezulu with her beaded hair and long slim body was so deep in his soul it twisted his stomach and put a smile on his face – all day long.

That morning he got up on the first shout from his dad downstairs.

Jonny, get a move on – it's 8 o'clock!

Time for that extra stare in the mirror – he made sure his hair was sleek and his teeth were sparkling, ready to go with his laid back walk into the school yard: in good time for a cool word with Win.

And bursting at his stitching with the fizz of being near her. Jonny Malone was one hopeless case.

9

If you like this song so much, you can sing it with us at the Taster next week.

The Taster was the night when new kids came to see if they wanted to come to the school the next September; when everyone showed off what a cracking place it was.

Jonny tried to put his voice way down there.

Eh, Win?

But rot it, he squeaked it out way up there.

If you say so.

Jonny spent all day going over those four little words, trying to find reasons for hope.

Show Time

Jonny couldn't get enough of rehearsals, never mind the doubts.

Just to be there with Win, doing this thing together, him 'doo-doo-doing' down in his chest, and this special girl by his side giving off vibrations which brought up goosebumps. He had to hang on to the mike to stay on his feet.

On the night of the Taster Jonny wore his party gear and gelled his dark hair so it shone under the stage lights. Belle, Charlee and Win looked like they'd shimmied straight out of the glossies. But no-one felt starry inside. Inside, they were their same scared old selves.

The hall was crowded. The new kids cheered when the lights went down and they screamed when the spots came on. And when the backing tape came beating out, the whole hall held its breath.

It was electric. Big kids went weak.
Teachers went dry in the mouth.
Two little girls in the front row
almost went to heaven.

Never mind the amps and speakers, it was the screaming and cheering that had the hall lights swinging.

The band had to do the song three times, and then autograph Taster Night programmes all the way out to the gate.

When the girls had gone off
in Belle's mum's car, Jonny
walked round in circles
for half an hour
saying,

Mr Malone has left
the building..!

He'd got to keep this
going. It was the best
thing that had ever
happened to him.
The acclaim. But
especially the getting
it next to Win.

Let's go pro

It had to be a demo
tape next. Wasn't
that always next on the
glittery road for a band?

And Mr Turner went for it, no messing.
He'd been knocked into the wall by the song
the night before, and he nodded so hard saying
yes his head nearly came off.

> Great! We'll lay down
> a track. That's what
> we'll *do* - lay down
> a track and *go*
> from there.

He went on about laying down a track to the point
where they wanted to lay him flat on his back.

So they did. And they went round telling everyone how real pros went direct to DAT. No mistake. They were going to be stars!

It wasn't till they were at Belle's house telling her mother about it all that they tumbled to something being missing.

Medium to Big Time

But if they'd thought they were going direct to the big time they were in for a downer. Studio 100 was in Bernie Falcon's house, round the corner from school. Getting out of Belle's mum's car in Herbert Street didn't quite have the same feel as pulling up in a stretch limo outside Abbey Road.

Mind that pushchair. And those wellies.

Not quite Reception, is it?

But down in the basement they were well impressed. The studio ran right under the house, with a big consul, all the computer stuff they'd seen on films, and a wide two inch tape machine which was real big time. Bernie Falcon tapped the consul.

Twenty-four tracks.

You ever recorded anyone big?

Any *Top of the Pops* people?

Loads. And what's 'big'? Everyone's project's big to them, isn't it?

He was a pro, Bernie. If you were in his studio you were important. Jonny remembered him from school plays when he'd come in to help Mr Turner with the sound effects.

You do the singing in here, on the other side of that glass partition.

Bernie pointed to where there were four microphones hanging up.

One mike each!

Oooer! Don't like the look of that!

Making a track each, now they'd hear how bad he really was...

But he was stood next to Win again, which was all he wanted out of life, and he was soon swept up with what Bernie and Mr Turner had been doing before the band got there.

Rapid's home-made backing track had been redone on the sampler, and it came out sounding really professional. Belle's mouth hung open.

Did I write that music?

That's your stuff, girl!

Wow! Didn't know it was any good!

But what the four of them sang to was just a drum rhythm and a thin keyboard melody line – each into their own mike, with a hand over one ear to look professional.

Three hours later, Bernie put two thumbs up through the glass partition.

We've cracked it, gang!

And Mr Turner was all smiles.

Real groovy!

It would all get put together in the mix. They were shown the DATs which would be made off the big tape – each about the size of a matchbox. And they were given cassettes of their morning's work.

Ups and Downs

Miracle! Only a week went by before they got the call. Mr Turner phoned Belle's mum.

Pace Records want to meet Rapid.

After Belle phoned Jonny to tell him the news he spent an hour practising his autograph. He reckoned he'd vary it according to whether it was for girls or boys... till he decided he was only ever going to claim 'love' for one person; the rest of the world would only ever get 'best wishes'.

Love
Jonny
XX

Best wishes
Jonny Malone

He went round to Win's house on a high of highs.
Not to stare into those eyes which sent him just
a little bit dizzy. Not to look at that mouth
he wanted to kiss when she was singing.
Just to make sure she knew about the
recording, of course. But when
he got there the news was bad.

Can't come.

We're going to Birmingham
that Saturday.

33

Belle's mum had a go at changing the date, but what they'd offered was what they'd offered. Pace Records twiddled all the knobs, thank you very much.

So the Saturday session had to be the Saturday session – with Pleasure Julien rehearsed and standing in for Win Bhekezulu. Not the day out Jonny had been dreaming of – for him and the girl he was crazy about.

Show Biz

When Saturday came, Belle's mother went with them, well briefed by Bernie Falcon on what to expect.

> Looks like they want you, you've got something there they thinks a 'kicker'. So don't fall over yourself with the first offer.

They were met by Honey Brown and Scott Martin. Honey Brown with lacquered hair and a hard edge, and Scott Martin with a pony tail and a soft smile.

They'd practised that morning, but Honey Brown didn't want them singing today. She wanted to talk copyright and ages and permissions.

She spoke to them like a teacher dishing out bad grades.

Belle's mum wanted the low-down.

So what's the score?

A possible one-off, like schools do recordings of carols at Christmas. Or covering it. Or –

Covering it? What's that, please?

Honey Brown looked at Scott Martin. It seemed the meeting was coming to its crucial point.

41

But Belle's mother was Belle's mother. It was going to be a 'no cover' deal with Rapid and her daughter or nothing.

Honey Brown and Scott Martin had a whole conversation with their eyes.

Okay, okay, we could talk along those lines.

Hold On!

There were hopeful smiles on several faces – on Belle's and her mother's, and on Charlee's.

But not on Jonny's – and from his mouth not a click, but a loud clear of his throat. Because now he was seeing what Win had been going on about. About attitudes.

Excuse me, but that's dead racist!

Belle's mother raised an eyebrow.

I beg your pardon?

Scott Martin was staring at Jonny – but with one of those looks which gave nothing away about what he was thinking. Anyhow, it shut Jonny up.

Honey Brown stood up.

Well, we'll have to leave it there. I expect you've all got a busy Saturday.

And with that she dismissed them back to their shopping.

If you can persuade Win to come along, I think we might be talking contract...

The drive home from the dream factory on the Great West Road was a bitter run.

Belle and her mother sat in the front, with Pleasure and Charlee next to each other in the back – and Jonny as tight into a corner as he could get himself. But that didn't stop the verbals.

Was that you going on in there, or Win? Cos it was well out of order without getting our say-so!

We're s'posed to be a band! You know? We're in it together.

And it's our song! Me and Charlee's — we wrote it.

Belle's mother nodded and gave Jonny the evil eye in the mirror. Jonny couldn't make himself any smaller. He'd stuck his nose well into where it hadn't been wanted.

Sorry.

Jonny shut his eyes to call up a picture of Win. But he couldn't.

No doubt fed up with just nodding, Belle's mother had her say.

The best you can do, you in the back, is get Win to go for it. There's a lot of other people riding on this.

And those people are interested. You tell her to look at it as an opportunity, and not be so defensive.

'Yeah!' everyone else said.
Except Pleasure Julien, of course.

Every Good Boy Deserves...

No-one told Win anything. It was left to Jonny, but he was leaving it too – especially when he had a special smile off her on the Monday.

What was Saturday like?

Not all that. But I hope your day was ace.

Yeah, it was great. All the family, people over from South Africa, an African band, special food.

And my auntie looking like the queen of all the world.

Wish I could've come.

Which he did wish – and the saying of it got him rewarded with a reply he'd never forget.

An' I wish you'd been there! Missed you. Got used to you bein' around.

I kep' thinking it would've been great, you bein' there.

Did she? Had she? Was this Christmas and birthday all rolled into one? Jonny couldn't say a thing for a bit, had to take a lean on the school railings. Just looking casual, like... Win was staring at him and the sights and sounds of the school yard disappeared.

51

They were both standing on a private cloud, Jonny's head scraping heaven. Finally he found his tongue.

You like pizza?

Some toppings.

Have one tonight? With me? Down Mangellos?

Be good.

See you there.

Six o'clock?

And the bell went, leaving Jonny to follow the tall slim back of Win Bhekezulu into school – on the wobbliest legs in the world.

Date!

Never mind Jonny's
worst fears that
the world might
come to a stop,
six o'clock did come
round. There was
just the getting out
of the house to do.

His dad looked at him with that twenty year
difference in his eyes, all dust, stubble and lumber-
jacket coming in from work, and Jonny all hair gel
and the pong of *Monsieur* going out.

Off down
the pit, son?

The usual touch. If you didn't look beefy you were dead meat in this house. A son with a recording contract would have really flattened his dad's beer.

Yeah, double shift. Where have you been? Just had your nails polished?

Fight fire with fire. He shot out of the door while his dad was still thinking up a lightning response.

Mangellos was a theme pizza place, all the seating set round a fairground's Galloping Horses. There were dodgem cars with tables on the bonnets for the twos, and revolving cups and saucers (which didn't revolve) for the groups. And tonight was one of the rare times Jonny had cause to go for a dodgem.

Go in here, shall we?

Him and Win, knee to knee in number seven.

It was definitely one of those can't-believe-your-luck times. Win had brushed her eyelids with sky blue, kissed her lips with pale pink, and threaded blue and pink beads into her hair to match.

Definitely on a wavelength, us.

Win smiled. Could be, sort of thing.

Like two mobile phones.

Nerves always made Jonny go on. What he'd said wasn't funny, but he snorted laughing, needed a tissue and wished he'd kept his cool.

He went up to the counter to order. It gave him time to think, because he hadn't planned anything beyond just being here. But now they were, it was real.

And if Win asked about the Rapid morning he'd leave that in the air. He wasn't into doing Belle's mum's dirty work. Then, he'd move on the chat to a possible trip to the Mega Bowl or the MGM Picture House, Saturday or Sunday... Meanwhile, just being here with Win, getting to know her, it still made breathing something he had to think about.

Large or regular?

Regular, please.

He'd never get a large one down.

Deep pan or thin crust?

He took a chance on deep pan. But only a chance, because, honest, wasn't there tons to learn about someone else? Someone you wanted to learn about.

Trouble!

But he'd hardly got back to the dodgem, hardly sorted his knees so they didn't touch Win's unless she did the touching, hardly opened his mouth to ask her more about Saturday in Birmingham, when who went past the window? Only Belle! Walking fast, going somewhere, chewing at her lips all agitato.

He shot his menu up to hide his face, but it was too late. Her eyes grew wide, and the lip chewing settled into a smile.

Of course she came in. She skipped round the galloping horses to their dodgem and sat on the back.

Hi!

Wotcha.

If only Jonny could stamp his foot on the fast pedal and go.

So – has he done it?

Done what?

Win's eyes flashed.

Done the business?

Belle looked at Jonny for support.

Listen... I...

But Belle wasn't waiting for any excuses.

Has he talked you round to coming to Pace with us. Told you how much we need you?

What!

Never did anyone ever
come so close to having
a Hawaiian in the face
and a banana milk
shake over the head.

Out On Your Ear

It came out at school next day – what Honey Brown had wanted. Jonny didn't want to hear, not with Win keeping the width of the school yard between them, but Charlee made sure he did, now he was out of the band.

They said forget the 'clicks', they can do things with the song as it is.

Another school band's all got 'flu, so they want Rapid back next Saturday.

Yeah, all dressed up to do a video on ds With Style – going out that night.

The finger of fate was doing its usual crooked pointing.

Win – now things didn't hang on her doing her clicks – said yes to rejoining the group. And Baz Young was subbed for Jonny.

He can easy doo-doo-doo as good as you.

So Rapid mark three was born, with Jonny Malone left for dead – out on his ear from the band, and with a flea in it from Win Bhekezulu.

What's On The Box?

It had to be Jonny's dad's sort of thing, didn't it? *Kids With Style.* He'd only just stopped taking the Beano.

You oughta watch this! Bit of talent for you...

Can't be bothered.

But, tough though it was, Jonny had to stand leaning on the back of an armchair – permanently on the way out of the room – to catch some of the show.

They were on early. Rapid. The girls looking great –
especially Win in braids, beads and robes, like her
aunties at the wedding.

And Jonny ached. He
ached badly; he ached
the ache of a three mile
cross-country run on top
of a hundred press-ups
and a kilometre swim –
the ache of love and
longing. Love and
longing for the girl in
his living room, singing
the song, and – now
that they weren't any
part of the deal – doing
her Zulu clicks.

A smile would have been more than Jonny's spirit could have managed, even to save his life. He pushed out of the room and dived up the stairs. He had to get out of the house and just shout, give the moon some stick.

And there was the song again, a close-up on Win, going by the sound of it.

They playing it again?

He came back down the stairs because he couldn't not. But the words weren't coming from the telly. These words were coming through the letter-box, and the door was being rapped.

Don't get

me wrong,

Don't go go

go away,

want you

all night long,

Don't go

go go

away...

Happy Endings

Jonny didn't let her in. He opened the door and went out to her. To Win. Well, his dad wouldn't cope with the telly coming to life, would he? That girl in his living room.

And Win turned him to face her, put her hands on his shoulders and kissed him on the lips.

He squeezed her hand; and, dream-time, she squeezed his. The best answer in the world.

They walked on down the pavement, his arm round her shoulder, her head leaning just a bit into him. And not much needed to be said.

79